FAKING IT WITH MY BROTHER'S BEST FRIEND

A Fake Relationship Romantic Comedy

MELISSA SCHROEDER

Edited by
NOEL VARNER

Cover Art by
SCOTT CARPENTER

Contents

About Faking it with my Brother's Best Friend   v
Friend
Acknowledgments   vii

CHAPTER ONE   1
Hazel

Chapter Two   11

CHAPTER THREE   19
Hazel

CHAPTER FOUR   27
Milo

CHAPTER FIVE   33
Hazel

CHAPTER SIX   41
Milo

CHAPTER SEVEN   49
Hazel

CHAPTER EIGHT   55
Milo

CHAPTER NINE   61
Hazel

CHAPTER TEN   67
Milo

CHAPTER ELEVEN   75
Hazel

CHAPTER TWELVE   85
Milo

Epilogue   91

Coming Next—> 99
The Melissa Schroeder Instalove Collection 101
About the Author 103
Also by Melissa Schroeder 105

About Faking it with my Brother's Best Friend

Part of the **Melissa Schroeder Instalove Collection**: *Same World. Any Order. Individual Love.*

I've been in love with Milo Darling for as long as I can remember.

He's my brother's best friend and would never be interested in a curvy girl like me. I've seen the women he's dated in the past, and let's just say they don't look like me. I've come to terms with it...mainly.

When I hear my ex is going to be at a charity ball I have to attend, the natural thing is to ask Milo. He's safe, and he's a gentleman, and well, who wouldn't want to spend the night with the most beautiful man ever created.

Only, he's not looking at me like I'm just a friend, and when he kisses me on the dance floor, I lose every thought

I have ever had in my life. And, yeah, maybe, I'm going to be okay with a one-night fling with the man of my dreams. Who can blame a girl for taking him up on his offer?

And that night? I will just say that it blows my world apart. But I know as soon as the sun rises, this girl will have to put on her big girl pants and get on with my life. Because there is one thing I understand and that's that girls like me don't get happily ever afters with guys like him.

Author Note: These two might start out thinking it's all fake, but well, you know how things go in the Instalove World. There's hijinks, a trip to a drag queen brunch, Milo in a tux, and scene in front of a mirror that embarrassed this author. As always with an Instalove Collection book, low drama, lots of romance, and a happily ever after.

Acknowledgments

Again, this book would not have happened without the help of my gang.

Thanks to Noel Varner for her editing skills and hard work.

Thanks to Scott Carpenter for another beautiful cover.

Addicts…What can I say? Y'all rock and your support always lifts me up.

To Brandy Walker and Joy Harris—thanks for always being there to help me work out all my issues. And I mean ALL MY ISSUES. There are many.

Thanks to all the reviewers and my Rough and Ready Review Group who help get the word out about my books. Without you, this would be much harder.

And of course, thanks to my family, Les and my girls. I have insane schedules and mood swings when a book is giving me issues. Thank you always for supporting me.

To Scott Carpenter who has given me so many beautiful covers over the last 17 years and is the genius behind the look of my Instalove Collection. Thank you, Cover God.

Chapter One

Hazel

"I'm not going."

My best friend and almost sister-in-law Georgie gives me a look. It's one I know well. Although she is five years younger than I am, she seems to have her life together. Hell, she's back in school and planning a wedding with my brother.

"You *are* going. You worked hard on this fundraiser and it's your baby. You are not letting that Rachel woman screw with you anymore."

Rachel Burton. She was my *Regina* in boarding school and college and made my life a living hell. The fact that our families knew each other made it worse. And now she's going to ruin everything once again. I mean, I should have known she was coming. She's searching for a husband, the richer the better. I'm pretty sure she doesn't care about love or even building a life together. Rachel has always worried about one thing and one thing only…herself.

A fundraiser event like the one I'm running next

weekend will be a great place for someone like her to be out on the hunt. I shouldn't care, truly. The things she did to me ended almost a decade ago, but she still gets to me. When I got the news about my ex showing up too, well, that just made it worse.

I realize I have been pacing back and forth in front of Georgie, who is sitting on the sofa in my office just watching me. I stop and cross my arms. I'm sure I don't look defensive at all. And my most recent pair of Louboutin's don't have a red sole.

"The best way to avoid that is not to go."

Silence fills the office as Georgie stares at me. Yes, I know I am almost twenty-eight years old, but I still haven't dealt with those issues from high school and college. I mean, I think I have most of the time, then I get smacked upside the head with another run in with Rachel or one of her crew. And to top everything off for the weekend of torture, I just found out my old college boyfriend, the one who slept with Rachel while he was still dating me, has RSVP'd to my fundraiser event. I didn't realize that he was invited, but I found out from Bastian my assistant that Jason is coming in place of his father.

"You said you were okay with going stag to the fundraiser you put together."

I frown harder. "I hate that term."

"What? Fundraiser?"

From the smirk on her face, I know she's screwing with me. "No. Stag. It's…"

"Something else to concentrate on rather than the fact that you have to get a date."

I sigh and collapse onto the sofa beside Georgie. I

don't say anything at first. We both know she is right, but I don't want to admit it. Of course, Georgie—being my best and only female friend—doesn't say a word. She patiently waits for me to respond. She knows me well. She used to be the receptionist here at Prescott, but now she's back in school and working on her business degree and getting married to my brother. And it was all thanks to me putting her together with my brother for a fake relationship.

I can wait her out. I'm good at it.

Less than thirty seconds passes before she says anything.

"Don't you have a guy friend you can take?"

I roll my eyes. "My guy friends are a little too...flamboyant I guess is the best word."

I know a lot of wonderful gay men. I mean A LOT. Until I met Georgie, they made up the majority of my friends. I know several who wouldn't think twice about stepping in to help. I just couldn't do that to any of them. Regina, I mean Rachel, is the worst. I would never ask my friends to be anything but what they are.

"Hey, how about Milo?"

My stomach tenses and my breathing hitches. Just hearing someone else say his name is enough to make me start babbling.

Milo Darling, my brother's best friend and all-around great guy. He's a sweetie who would do it, but I don't know if I could survive that. I've had a crush on Milo for years. I can't even remember when it started. All I know is whenever I think about him, or someone mentions his name, just anything to do with him really, my nipples get hard.

"He's too busy." He runs Darling Resorts and I know first-hand just how hard that is.

"No, he isn't. In fact, he's here in the building and coming over to talk to you."

"What?"

"He was hanging out with Silas, and I texted your brother to have Milo come over." While I had been pacing and ranting, she had apparently been texting. She seems sweet, but the woman is a little too smart for her own good.

Then I process what she says and panic hits me square in the chest as I try my best to catch my breath. "I can't do this."

"Do what? Talk to an old friend?"

There is a tone in her voice that tells me she knows about my crush. It's hard to hide it from my bestie, but still, it's embarrassing. He's the man I compare all other men to.

She leans closer and nudges me with her elbow. "You know he'll do it."

"And everyone will know it's a pity date."

"Hazel Prescott! There is no pity in going on a date with you."

I know she's right. I've come a long way in the last few years. I'm what they call curvy, and it has taken me a while to deal with what high school and college did to my head. It's one of the reasons I wear four-inch-heels even though I'm five ten. I love them and everyone else can just suck it.

"I know that, but...you've seen Milo."

"Yeah, I have. And I have seen the way he looks at you."

I roll my eyes. She's convinced Milo has a crush on me, but please...the man really is an Adonis, beautiful on the outside and, more importantly, on the inside. He is the CEO of Darling Resorts and, yes, he fits his name. Dark brown hair, green eyes, and he's tall. At six-four, he makes me feel tiny next to him. I love that about him.

There's a knock at my door before my brother steps in. I frown at him until I see Milo standing behind him. His gaze is searing. It's like that every time I see him, but I think that's Milo. He pulls people in easily and is one of the reasons he makes a good CEO. I have no doubt that if he hadn't been born into a wealthy family, he would be CEO of some other corporation. There's just something about Milo that draws people in. Which is why his friendship with my brother is so funny. He's the opposite of Silas.

"Georgie," my used to be not affectionate at all brother Silas says as he lifts his girlfriend off the couch and kisses her. A few months ago, I would call the doctor to get Silas an appointment at this behavior, but that's what falling in love did for him.

He sets her down on the floor. "So, what did you need?"

"She needs to talk to Milo."

"Yeah, so what do you need?"

"Remember when you asked me to tell you when you're being insensitive?" Georgie asks him gently.

"Yes."

"This is one of those times."

"Why? I was having a great time with Milo—"

"That's a lie. You were complaining that Georgie was spending time with your sister," Milo says, smiling, showing off those delicious dimples.

"I take it back. I don't want you to be my best man."

Milo's response is a wider smile. He knows my brother isn't being serious, although a lot of people would think he is. They are definitely night and day with their personalities, but they understand each other. That's what's important in a friendship. Georgie and I are completely different too. She's about five inches shorter than me, is sweet as can be, and is a brainiac. Like the things you need to use the calculator on your phone to figure out, she does it in her head. I'm good at more creative things, but we understand each other.

"Let's go, Silas."

"Why?"

She rises up to her tiptoes and whispers in his ear. His face changes from confusion to determination. He takes Georgie by the hand and starts dragging her out of the office.

"See ya later, Milo."

"Bye," Georgie calls back as she follows my brother out the door.

Silence descends on the room. I stand there looking like the dork that I am. It's hard not to. He's perfect and pretty. Really, really pretty.

Milo is just staring at me with those clear green eyes of his and I want to sigh. I don't because then he will know about my little infatuation with him. That would be embarrassing.

"So, you needed me?"

I curl my toes inside my Manolo Blahnik Mary Jane snakeskin pumps as his voice rumbles over the syllables of his question. I know it's my imagination, but God, it sounds like his tone deepens over each word. Does he sound like that in bed?

"Hazel?"

I blink and realize I've been staring at him like a goober. There is a good chance a little drool has dripped out of my mouth.

"Sorry. And I didn't call you down here, Georgie did."

He frowns. And yep, even that's sexy. I mean, a man that pretty while frowning just makes me want to make him smile, mainly while we are both naked.

Good god, I need to get my mind back on track.

"I thought it was you."

He sounds like a little boy who has been kept from his favorite treat. I sigh.

"Well, she did it for me without asking me beforehand."

"Oh."

He came anyway, and I need to say something, or this will get even more awkward. "Okay, now, I don't want you to think that I've lost my mind, but I have this thing next weekend, and I kind of need a date. Georgie suggested you for my date." My face is burning up as I babble on. "I mean, I understand if you don't want to go with me. It's a fundraiser for the charity Momzilla and I started, which means getting dressed up and pretending you want to be there with me."

He doesn't say anything for a long moment, and I

can't figure out what his expression means. It's oddly blank.

"I know it's kind of a pain. But I know you RSVP'd as part of Darling Resorts, and I know you don't always go to things of this sort. Since you're already going to come, I just thought you could pretend to be with me while you're there. Also, now I feel kind of like an idiot because you are certainly aware that it's downtown at your hotel. Still, if you are too busy, I promise not to hold it against you."

I snap my mouth shut. He's staring at me as if trying to figure out what I said, like I was speaking a foreign language.

"Why now?"

I blink again. "What?"

"Why now? You've known you had this event for a few months."

I sigh again. "I put it off."

"Hazel."

His tone tells me that he doesn't believe me. I just don't want to admit why I'm panicking right now. I hate feeling like this and despise even more caring about it.

"Okay there was that, but I was planning on going on my own, only…Rachel Burton is going to be there."

"And?"

God, he knows me too well. Maybe Ricky can pretend to be infatuated with me if I talk in a deeper voice. He would do it because he loves me, and, well, he would be really good at getting people to give up the goods. Of course, most people know who he is since he owns the number one drag queen spot in the city, so that probably wouldn't work.

"Hazel," he says, snapping his fingers in front of me. When did he get that close? He's looking down at me like…well, I don't know what. There is a mixture of irritation in his gaze but something deeper, something that has me squeezing my thighs together. Also, I know I can't lie to him.

"Jason's going to be there."

Chapter Two

I stare at the woman I've been half in love with for the last few years, and I realize she wants to use me against her college boyfriend. And right at this moment, I don't know how to feel about it.

"Jason? The guy you dated in college?"

She nods. "He messaged me yesterday on Facebook saying he wanted to catch up with me this weekend."

Great. This is the guy who broke her heart in college. I'm not sure what happened, but I do know that she doesn't date these days. She might say she's too busy with work, but I know better. And I know I have been fucking lucky that she hasn't been going out without me. I'm not sure I could handle that. Hazel is more than just a pretty face. She has a fascinating mind, and the sweetest freaking heart known to man.

"Listen," she says, moving her hands around. She loves to talk with her hands. "It's too much. Ricky has what he calls his heterosexual look clothes. He can pretend to be my boyfriend if I promise him a spa day."

Ricky is one of her drag queen friends, and he would do it. He's completely devoted to her like the others from his restaurant. At least I know he wouldn't pull anything on her because his husband would probably cut his balls off. I still can't let another man take my place. Not when I can use this situation to my benefit.

"I'll do it."

She pauses in her babbling, her dark brown eyes widening. "You will?"

God, she sounds like she expected me to turn her down. The truth is, I would crawl across broken glass for this woman. She has no idea, I'm sure of that, and if I didn't already think that her reaction would tell me.

"Yeah, I'll do it. I was already planning on going."

The sigh of relief that escapes her irritates me. What the fuck did that asshole do to my girl? And yes, I think of her as my girl because she always will be. I just needed the right opportunity to make her mine, and she's handed it to me on a silver platter.

"Thank you, Milo. I'll really owe you after this."

I shake my head. "No. I owe you and Silas. You both kept me sane these last few years."

It's the truth. I always expected to take over the family resort business, but the gravity of handling the business that supports so many of my relatives overwhelmed me. Silas and Hazel stepped up and helped me through it all. And yeah, Silas helped, but it was during that time that I realized that Hazel was meant for me.

Unfortunately, she has had me in the friend zone for all that time, but this situation will allow me to change that. I should feel guilty about using this situation to my advantage, but I refuse to let this chance pass me by.

"Thanks, Milo."

I nod. "Text me all the stuff I need to know. I need to talk to Silas about something, but we can chat Sunday at brunch?"

Gertrude's is one of the hottest brunch spots in the city but thanks to Hazel's connections to several of the drag queens who work there—and Ricky who owns it with his husband—Hazel has a standing reservation.

Thankfully, she doesn't realize I'm lying. I just spent thirty minutes with my best friend. Mostly, he complained that Georgie wasn't in his office, but if I had wanted to talk to him about something, I could have brought it up then.

No, I need to talk to Georgie because I definitely need some help.

Hazel offers me a blinding smile, one that I feel all the way to the tips of my toes. This woman. She gets my engine revving with just a smile. I can't even think about what she'll do to me while she's beneath me and I'm riding her hard.

Fuck. Now I'm getting hard and there are not a lot of ways to hide it.

"That sounds fabulous," she says.

"Text me the time and I'll be there."

She nods and smiles at me. And before I can embarrass myself, I leave her, my entire body buzzing from the experience of being with Hazel alone.

I make my way across the building to Silas' office

without talking to anyone. A few people wave, but I don't stop because I have one mission on my mind now.

"Is Georgie still in there with him?" I ask his assistant Brent.

He nods, so I knock, knowing the way those two are, they could be naked in his office.

"What?" Silas yells out.

"Silas," Georgie says. "Come in, Milo."

Of course she knew I was coming over here. I turn the knob and find it unlocked. When I step in, Georgie is sitting in his lap behind the desk.

"How did you know it was me?"

"Because Silas is being a real grump today and no one wants to deal with him," she says with a smile.

Silas tosses his fiancé a look, then zeroes in on me. "What did my sister want?"

"She wants me to go to the fundraiser thing she has next weekend."

"We are all going to that, right?" Silas asks Georgie. She nods but she doesn't seem surprised. It was her idea after all.

"And thanks for suggesting it."

She offers me a huge smile. She's a cute woman, tiny compared to Silas and always makes people think of fairies. And, while he is still a bit of an asshole to people, she has softened his rough edges.

"I thought it was a perfect opportunity for you to make your move. I mean…how long have you liked her?"

I shake my head as I feel my neck getting hot. There's no way I am going to admit that. "Has she said anything about me?

"What is this, high school?" Silas grumbles. Probably because there is a good chance that I cock-blocked him.

Georgie tosses her fiancé a look, then stands up to walk over to me. My idiot friend growls, but we both ignore him.

"I can't betray a confidence."

I nod, a little sad that she can't, but I understand.

"I will say that she is going to have a bad weekend if you aren't there. That Rachel—well, we know how I feel about her."

I nod. Rachel tried to break up Georgie and Silas when they first got together.

"And Jason…he was the worst. I don't know why he's coming, but she's been kind of a mess since he messaged her."

"Jason Knowles?"

Georgie looks back at Silas. "Yeah. She dated him in college."

I know Jason Knowles. Even before I knew he broke her heart, I didn't like the man. He's kind of smarmy and tends to make bad business deals. At the end of the day, he walks away richer and everyone else involved is usually bankrupt.

"Why did she date him? He sucks," Silas says voicing my opinion of him. His family are hedge fund managers, and they are known for being horrible in business. They've gotten in trouble with the SEC several times, and they can't keep employees around either.

"People don't always make the best choices in college. And you know your sister wasn't really good with men.

Going to an all-girls school didn't prepare her for college boys."

True. I drank way too much in college. Hell, there are nights I can't even remember, but all that changed when my dad had his heart attack and I had to take over the business when he retired.

"So, I said we would have brunch Sunday at Gertrude's."

Georgie jumps and claps. "Yay. I love that place."

"I do not."

I frown at Silas, then look back at Georgie. She shakes her head. "I told you they flirt with everyone."

"I have no problem with flirting. I have a problem when they get handsy. I do not appreciate being manhandled."

I snort.

His gaze zeroes in on me. Most people would freak out because, well, Silas is blunt as fuck. But I know better. And I am totally delighted by the situation.

"Shut up. You have no idea."

"I do. In fact, Lucy has a crush on me. Of course, I'm comfortable enough in my manliness to appreciate a little flirting."

"It wasn't just flirting. I told you. It was a pinch, and she had the nerve to give me her number."

I laugh knowing that Silas isn't transphobic or homophobic. He would be appalled if anyone did that to him. Well, anyone but Georgie. He's got issues, more than I do. But thankfully, Georgie took care of that.

"So, you have a plan for this weekend?" Georgie asks sitting on Silas' desk.

I shove my hands into my pockets and try my best to hide my true thoughts. If I had my way, it would just be the two of us and a bed. That's all I need.

Blurting that out would be embarrassing and crass seeing that Silas is Hazel's brother.

"Not sure. They're having it at the Premiere Darling."

Yeah, it's a bit weird, but our last name is a big seller, and even after all these years, it's odd to me to say it out loud. Like I'm talking in third person.

"You should get one of the suites and surprise her," Georgie suggests.

"Yeah?"

She nods.

"Okay, well, I have a few meetings later today, so I'm going to head that way. Gertrude's on Sunday, right?"

"Yes. Now go." Silas can be such an ass. And just to screw with him, I lean forward and brush my mouth over her Georgie's cheek. When I pull back, her eyes are twinkling. She gets what I'm doing.

"Next time you do that, I will punch you in the balls," Silas says as he rounds the desk.

I just laugh as I head out of his office. I have a plan and that makes everything better. If all goes well, I will finally tell Hazel how I feel.

Chapter Three

Hazel

I apply my lip gloss and study myself in the mirror. I have always felt I was too big…too much. My weight has never bothered me. No, I take that back. It has bothered me in the past, but mostly when I'm with women. I was the first in my year group to get boobs, which Rachel claimed was because of my weight. It wasn't until I went to UVA that I found out just how much men loved boobs and I began to understand Rachel's attacks had more to do with what she saw as her inadequacies.

So I know men like my shape, or some men at least. It's that I'm almost six feet tall and men find that intimidating. I know, I know. Men say they want a tall woman, blah blah blah. Not true. Not when they're standing beside me. I have been on just a few dates in the last year, and all of them asked me why I wore stilettos.

Because I want to, asshole.

"Prince Charming has arrived."

I look at Ricky in the mirror. We met one day when I came in feeling lonely, unable to find my place at the company. I wanted to prove myself, but could never seem to find the right fit, until I took over the marketing. I understand what people want and I know how to get them to desire it.

"Who would that be?"

He rolls his eyes. Next to Georgie, Ricky is my best friend. He's known me longer, but now that he's married, he doesn't have as much time for me. Of course, now that Georgie is engaged to my brother and expecting their first child, she will start to be too busy for me.

And now I feel horrible for being jealous of my friends. I'm the one who set up Silas and Georgie.

"That would be Mr. Milo, and he asked after you already."

I'm in the back where the drag queens wander around in various states of undress. It's nothing new for me. I feel more comfortable here than I do in high society, and I've spent my whole life there.

"And you are going to knock his socks off, *mamacita*."

I stand back from the mirror and look at myself. It took me years to learn how to dress to enhance my curves. I usually opt for maxi dresses because I like the way they look and they are so darned comfortable. The floral print I am wearing today cinches in at the waist, accenting my hourglass figure. The vibrant colors bring out the gold in my brown eyes and make my hair appear even darker.

"He is going to be like one of those cartoon characters whose eyes pop out of their heads."

It's my turn to roll my eyes. "Sure."

His eyes narrow and he moves so he's in front of me.

"Do *not* make me mad. You know what happens, and then I will tell Francie it was your fault."

When Ricky gets mad, he consumes enough carbs for all of the city. For a month. And then he bloats up and Francie has to deal with the fallout. Francie being his husband and star of Gertrude's.

"Fine. It's just, I know he's doing this as a favor to my brother and my family."

"And you. Girl, he wants you. I know that you don't believe me, but he does."

"I have to agree."

Georgie's standing there smiling at me. She's got her hair up in two buns and is dressed down in a pair of jeans and cute tank top. I, of course, am overdressed because I always get too dressed up.

"What?" She asks, her smile fading.

"Nothing. I feel overdressed."

"Jesus in a skirt, woman, you are not overdressed. You look like a goddess, as you always do. It's your skanky friend who is underdressed."

"Hey," Georgie says, but she's laughing. She knows Ricky is just messing with her.

"Come on. Get out there and have a nice brunch."

I sigh and rise from the seat.

"Go, get him girl," Lucy calls out. There are more catcalls and I let one eyebrow rise up.

"Okay, I know you told me not to tell anyone, but I couldn't help it. I wanted to have all the good thoughts coming your way, and you know my girls can make mountains move."

"Fine, but you owe me a pedicure date."

We head out to find both Silas and Milo sitting in the booth. Silas looks more than a little agitated, but I see his expression calm when he sees Georgie. Just that look right there is what I want, what I need in my life.

I move my gaze over to Milo, expecting to see him talking to one of the many queens who are giving him attention. Instead, I find his attention zeroed in on me. There seems to be a flare of heat in the depths of his green gaze that sends heat lapping through my blood. My nipples tighten as I feel all the liquid heat in my stomach drop to my sex. God, that man. I know that he's just looking at me, but my body is raring to go for a bout of hot, sweaty sex.

I blink that thought away. I've had one experience with a man, and that was horrible. I hated it, and I swore that it would take me a miracle to want to do that again. Well, not a miracle, but a very patient man who knows what he's doing. And I am sure Milo is good at that, but still. I have a rule. Or I did. I don't know any more because here I am, Milo looks at me, bats his eyes, and I'm ready to jump him.

"Go," Ricky says, poking me in the back.

"Rude," I say as Georgie slips her arm through mine and we make our way over to one of the best seats in the house. Sometimes it pays to be good friends with the owner of the hottest brunch place in town.

"He was really nervous when we got here," Georgie says to me in a tone that I know she thinks is quiet, but it isn't. She's a tiny woman, but she has a mighty voice.

"Who was flirting with him this time?"

All the ladies here love him. Mainly because Milo flirts back. That and they all go gaga over his stupid eyelashes.

"No one. Well, all of them, but he was agitated that you weren't out here. Once Ricky told him you were here and he would come get you, Milo calmed down."

As we come up to the table, I study the man I've known most of my life in some way or another. And yes, I had a crush on him, but I did on a lot of the guys I knew then. It wasn't until he took over Darling Resorts that we really became friends.

"About damned time," Silas says, as he stands to let Georgie slip into the booth. It's one of those horseshoe style ones. The bench is fuchsia, the table white. And I love it. It should be garish, but come on, this is a drag queen restaurant. It's supposed to be over the top.

"So romantic, Silas," I say, as Milo stands and lets me do the same as Georgie so we're sitting next to each other. When he slips back into the booth, though, he scoots a little closer than he normally sits.

Silas opens his mouth, probably to say something horrible to me, but Lucy shows up to take our orders. Georgie goes for a virgin daiquiri, both Silas and Milo order coffee, and I get a mimosa. Because it's brunch and there is no way I am passing up the opportunity to order alcohol for breakfast.

"So next weekend, you have this thing?" Milo asks.

I nod. "I'm the head of the silent auction committee, and I thought about taking Ricky because that is the sort of thing he loves. He really is good at raising money for good causes."

He can be a bit cutthroat with silent auctions. He'll

zero in on people who both want the same thing and start a battle over whatever they want. It drives the price up and then; the charity makes so much more money. The added benefit is that Ricky loves sticking it to rich people.

"But your ex is going to be there?"

"Yeah, I want to avoid him as much as possible."

"He sounds like a jerk," Georgie says.

"I know. You don't have to remind me how stupid I was in college." I turn back to Milo. Did he get closer? God, he smells so good. I lick my lips trying to gather my thoughts and he follows the movement with his gaze. My heart starts to speed up and heat fills my face. "He's been messaging me, and I have no idea why."

"I do." Milo's murmur is hard to hear above the noise of the brunch crowd. In fact, it's so soft, I think I might have just imagined it.

"Then there's Rachel Burton."

"Regina!" Georgie exclaims.

"Like in *Mean Girls*," Milo says.

My eyes widen. "You know *Mean Girls*?"

He scoffs. "Of course. One of the best movies of all time."

We share a smile, and that is a point in his favor.

"What the hell is *Mean Girls*?" Silas mutters.

"Silas Prescott don't tell me you haven't watched one of the most quotable movies of all times," Lucy says as she brings us our drinks. "I guess we should set up a movie date."

"Only if Georgie can come on the date."

"Oh, sweetie, I didn't know you were swingers."

I snort and Georgie giggles. Silas gives Lucy the stink

eye. We give her our food order then. I always get the same thing since their stuffed French toast is a miracle of carbs.

"So, that's why. Plus, it will be easier to work the room with you there. Some of the old guys are kind of…handsy."

Anger moves over his face. "Who?"

I blink at the change of demeanor. Milo is usually so nice and calm. Right now, he looks ready to commit murder. I don't think I've ever seen him this mad before.

"No one in particular. I have avoided them, thankfully, because Silas would come with me. Everyone's afraid of him."

Milo frowns but gives me a nod. I thought he was irresistible when he smiled at me, but that frown…well, it demolished my panties. I hope he can't see my nipples through my layers of clothing. I could say it was the air conditioning, then I realize it wouldn't come up in the conversation unless I said something about it. And that would be awkward, especially with Silas and Georgie here.

"So, tell me about this charity," he says, his expression clearing a little.

I push aside those other feelings and thoughts and tell him about the charity. He wasn't trying to turn me on. He was just playing the big brother and the sooner I can accept that, the sooner I can move on from my stupid little crush and find someone who can really love me.

Chapter Four

Milo

As I listen to Hazel speak, I lose track of everyone else. It's like this when we're around other people. I don't care about anyone else in the area, just my girl.

She's especially delectable today. I love the long maxi dresses she wears. They always cling to her body in the most amazing ways, and there is always cleavage showing. I try my best not to stare, but all I can think about is sucking on her nipples before sliding my dick between them.

There's a sparkle to her when she talks about the work she does, whether it's for the business or her charities. And I know a lot of rich women are involved in charities, but not the way Hazel is. She gets her hands dirty, as she likes to say. She doesn't just show up on holidays to have her picture taken. She will be at a shelter on a Wednesday because they needed her. Or she might be working at the food kitchen on a Saturday morning just because.

I scoot closer when she isn't looking at me and draw in

her earthy scent. There's a hint of roses, but an underlying scent that I know is unique to Hazel. I want to nuzzle her neck and draw it in.

"So, what we do is pull our resources together to raise money. Then the board works with the women's shelters to find out what kind of things they need. We get a lot more exposure this way."

"That's actually pretty brilliant," Georgie says. Hazel's face flushes.

"Thank you. I wasn't the only one who came up with it."

"How long have you been running this charity?" I ask. I know a lot about Hazel, but she does so much other work outside of her regular job at Prescott Enterprises.

"I'm not in charge," she says with a chuckle. "Momzilla and I have been working on this idea with a few of the shelters for a few years. We went live last year. I'm head of raising money. I'm supposed to just handle all the outreach because I'm good at that, but I excel at fundraising. We're doing a fundraiser here in a couple of months."

"And you added a few more shelters, right?" Georgie asks.

Hazel smiles at her friend, and I can't fight the smile that curves my lips. I can't help that when she's happy I am happy. It's just the way my world works these days.

"So what goes on at this fundraiser?"

She turns back to me, and the air backs up in my throat. It's like this every damned time. At least since I started noticing her. Yes, we've known each other a long time, but it took me awhile to move her out of the little sister of my best friend category. I can remember the precise moment it hit me that I was in love with her. We were working late on a marketing campaign she helped me with for our massive resort in the Shenandoah Valley. We were sitting at a table together, just like this, but not as close, and she smiled at me. That's it. That's all I needed, and I knew I was in love with her.

"We have a silent auction, some Scooby snacks, and an open bar—thanks to the generous CEO of Darling resorts."

I tip my head in acknowledgment; although, I had no idea we did that. My staff knows to give Hazel just about anything she wants.

"I'm mainly in charge of the silent auction. That's been kind of fun. Last year we went with traditional things, but this year, we had a lot of businesses jump on board."

"Did you get something from that bakery I like?" Georgie asks.

It takes a long second before Hazel pulls her gaze from mine. I draw in a deep breath, as my heart is beating out of control. I am in my thirties and I, unfortunately, spent my early twenties mostly drunk and having one-night stands. A woman has never affected me this way. It's like if I can't see her on a regular basis, I'm afraid I might just stop existing.

"Yes, I did."

"You will have to bid on that, Silas," she orders Silas.

My former uptight friend doesn't explode like he would have a year ago or if anyone else suggested that he bid on the package. He shrugs. "Okay."

From the moment he met Georgie, he's been like this. He would do anything for her, and I understand that feeling. I would move heaven and earth if Hazel said it would make her happy.

She turns back to face me with a smile curving her lips. "And we got a very generous weekend package from Darling Resorts."

"I told them to give you whatever you wanted."

Her smile widens into a grin. "I know. And I'm not sure Theo is going to be happy about it, but Allegra said it was something new she wants to offer."

Our new food and beverage manager for the resort and my brother Theo have been knocking heads since I hired her. He's the head chef for the resort and crafts most of our menus, and he does not take orders well.

"Oh, I would love to get a cooking lesson from Theo," Georgie says.

"No. Absolutely not," Silas says, his usual frown turning darker.

"Why not?"

"Just because."

I know why Silas doesn't want Georgie near my brother. I was a reprobate during my early twenties, and Theo still is. He's a womanizer in the worst sense, and while I don't usually judge people, I will say that a man looking at thirty should at least be settling down a little.

Truthfully, I know he could try anything on Georgie, and she wouldn't want to have anything to do with him. Silas is her man, and I don't see that changing. And while there are always rumors, I know that they aren't true.

Theo doesn't poach. Doesn't mean he wouldn't flirt with Georgie to drive Silas crazy.

"I would too. I am so bad in the kitchen," Hazel says.

All my thoughts of my brother not poaching are thrown out the window. There is no way she is getting near Theo. I open my mouth to say that, then I realize I have no right to give her orders.

"Not sure how much fun it would be to cook with my brother. Since I have a feeling he might not agree to do it."

Her smile fades. "Do you think he would refuse?"

"No. He will do it. But with you being a family friend, he might not curb his comments."

Her expression lightens a bit. "Oh, okay. I want to make sure the person who pays for the lesson gets what they paid for."

"They will. I will make sure of it."

She smiles at me again, and I can't help the small sigh that escapes. One of these days she will smile at me like that, the only difference is that we will both be naked and in my bed.

My cock twitches at the thought and I beat back my need. Just a week and I will make sure I take my chance with her.

Hazel

"So, do you have everything I gave you on all of the top donors from last year?" I ask.

Ricky rolls his eyes. He offered to come over and help me get ready since my assistant has the flu.

"You've asked me five times and what did I say the other four times?'

I sigh and shove my hand through my hair, wincing when I hit a nasty knot.

"And quit doing that. You're making a mess of yourself," he says, tsking.

I know I am. I mean, I'm dealing with so much pent-up need. All for Milo. My entire body is still vibrating and every time he texts me, my heartbeat speeds up. At this rate, I'm worried my heart is going to burst out of my body.

I inwardly groan. After spending time with my trusty vibrator—and, yes, I called Milo's name out when I came —I promised myself I would put any ideas of the two of us out of my mind. I have one day left before the fundraiser.

"What does it matter if I look like a mess?"

It's a good question because we're at my apartment today. With everything I need to double check on with the event, I decided to take a day off. If there was an issue, I can take care of it from here. But I need a strategy.

"I have to look at you. Do you think I want to see a mess?"

There are times I wonder why we're friends. I mean, we shouldn't work on paper, but we do. I call him my gay boyfriend and I'm his straight girlfriend. But he's more than that really. I have a very small group of friends—true friends. You know the kind I mean. The ones who know your secrets and if you needed them at one in the morning, you could call them.

He's come to a lot of my fundraisers, and normally he would be there tomorrow night. Just as a friend, because everyone knows who Ricky Garcia is in this town. The rich and powerful always show up at his restaurant, whether they want to admit it or not. Unfortunately, I couldn't ask him. It just so happened that it landed on his wedding anniversary.

"And stop looking at me like that. I am not going to the fundraiser."

"It's okay. Georgie will be there."

"I will!" Georgie says running into the room.

"Hey, slow down. If you fall down in my apartment and Silas hears about it, he'll blame me."

She rolls her eyes. "Be right back."

She hurries off to the bathroom. She seems to be

doing that a lot lately, I think with a tinge of envy. I'm ecstatic that I'm going to have a niece or nephew. It's just that I don't think it is ever going to happen for me. But that's what happens when you fall for a man who is out of your league.

My phone buzzes and I snap it up. I've been worried Milo is going to come to his senses and back out of this insanity.

Momzilla: *Do you want to ride together to the fundraiser?*

Me: *No. I have to be there at about two in the afternoon, and I doubt you will want to be there that early.*

Momzilla: *That's nap time.*

I chuckle. My mom has been loving life since Dad retired. He worked so hard for so many years, but the moment he handed everything over to Silas, his main focus was my mother. And I have a feeling my dad takes those naps with my mom, if you get my drift.

That's what I want. I want a man who wants nothing more than to be with me and enjoy my company. I've had crap luck dealing with that.

"What are you wearing tomorrow night?" Georgie asks as she settles on the big, overstuffed chair, her hands on her stomach. She already acts like she has a baby bump, which she doesn't. It's kind of cute and goofy at the same time.

"I was thinking the red dress."

"Girl, you have fifty million red dresses," Ricky says.

That's true. It is my favorite color.

"You mean the one with the big split up to your vajay-jay?" Georgie asks.

"It isn't…it's just high thigh."

Ricky stops what he's doing and stares at me. "You mean the one I have been begging you to wear for the last five months. The one that new designer made for you, saying that he thought you were the perfect model?'

"Oh, that Italian guy?" Georgie asks. "He had the hots for you." She wiggles her eyebrows and I blush.

"He did not. He was just trying to get in good here in the states."

"Sorry, but all men are the same, whether they are going after men or women, and I agree with Georgie. That man wanted you."

I blink at Ricky. Georgie isn't any better with men than I am. I had one relationship and one sexual experience in my past. She had none. But Ricky, he definitely knows men.

"How do you know that?"

"Darling, he watched you move. And he was overly interested in your tits."

I glance down and then shake my head before frowning at him. "All men—" he opens his mouth, but I plow ahead, "all heterosexual men, that is, look at my boobs. It's automatic."

"And your ass. He looked at your ass a lot. Plus, he asked me if you were seeing anyone."

"Wait, what?"

"I was right!" Georgie yells and dances around my living room before losing her balance and falling. Thankfully, it's on the couch.

"He did. I told him you were involved."

I settle my hands on my hips. "Why did you do that?"

"Because. You can't be involved with another man until you get Milo out of your system,"

"I don't want him out of my system."

"Exactly."

That's when I realized what I said. "I mean, he's not in my system. Other than a friend. A friend with really large hands."

He stands up. "Listen, I love you as much as I can since you have the wrong body parts. But, sweetie, you've been in love with him for years. When are you going to take a chance?"

I sigh and look at Georgie, who is watching us with rapt attention, as if we're a telenovela and the villain has just been revealed.

"I did that once. I fell on my face."

He steps closer and slings his arm around me. "You made a mistake in loving someone who wasn't worthy. You were young. You do not even want to know some of the mistakes I made in my early twenties."

"No, but you tell me about them anyway."

"I want to know about them," Georgie chimes in but he ignores her.

"This is what I am going to do. I am going to show up tomorrow. I am going to help you get ready before the fundraiser."

"No. You have plans."

"They aren't until later. I'm sure the hotel will let you have a room to stage things, so get hold of lover boy and find out."

I hesitate, but Georgie jumps in.

"It makes sense. You don't want to go there all dressed

up and you can't get ready for something like this in a bathroom. Text or call Milo. He'll help you. You know he will."

I nod and pull out my phone, knowing if I don't do this right now, I'll lose my nerve.

Me: *Hey, do you think I can get a room to get ready in tomorrow? I need to be there early and then I'll need to dress for the evening.*

Milo: *You got it. We have a family apartment you can use.*

"So?"

I look up at Ricky and Georgie. "Yeah. They apparently have some kind of apartment I can use."

My phone vibrates one more time and I look down.

Milo: *You can just store your things there until after the function.*

Ricky grabs the phone out of my hand.

"Hey!"

"Oh, baby, so we need all your stuff and some really great lingerie. White." He looks up at me. "Do you have white?"

"Isn't that boring?"

"Oh, no. It's makes the guys think of innocence. With that red dress you're going to wear…Milo will lose it," Georgie says. I almost open my mouth and ask how she knows that, but from the look in her eyes, it has something to do with my brother. I am super close with my brother, but I do have my limits.

"Okay," I say, as Ricky turns and heads back to my bedroom.

"Don't start going through my panty drawer."

He laughs. "No woman has ever accused me of that." But he doesn't stop. I hurry after him.

"Get a bag, and let's get you packed up for tomorrow."

I open my mouth to tell him to step off, but Georgie slips into my bedroom behind me.

"Just go along with Ricky on this one. I have a feeling he has a plan."

I look down at her. Georgie is super short. "I'm the one who plans."

"But we love you, baby girl, and for once, you should let your friends handle it," Ricky says.

He's standing there, holding one of my favorite bra and panty sets, and he should look ridiculous. But he doesn't. He's telling me he loves me in his own way. I look at Georgie and I feel the backs of my eyes burning.

"I swear if you start crying, I am going to lose it," Ricky says, his voice heavy with emotion.

I nod. "Thank you. Both of you."

"That's what friends are for," Georgie says. And with that, we start packing my clothes and getting me ready to go after the one man I think I might ever be able to truly love.

Milo

I draw in a deep breath, the scent of Hazel filling my senses. I know it's been hours since she was in my family's apartment at the hotel, but I can still sense her here. She has a small bag sitting on the chair in the living area that I'm sure is filled with all kinds of things, but I fought the need to zip it open and invade her privacy. Barely.

I finish tying my bowtie and step back from the bathroom vanity. I take in my appearance, making sure not a hair or thread is out of place. This is the night I stop being a pussy and go after the woman I love.

I try to remember the moment I realized I was in love with her. When my father got sick a few years ago and the doctor suggested he retire, I was twenty-seven years old and not ready to take over the company. I had trained for it, worked my way up in the company like the entire family is expected, but emotionally I wasn't ready. I thought I had years left before I had to deal with our company. But then Dad had his heart attack and that was that. I had spent a huge part of my twenties fucking around, drinking, spending time with people who I should never want anything to do with.

Then the heart attack happened. I had been halfway across the world and the trip back had sobered me right up. The weight of everything I had to handle almost broke me at that point. My family depends on our resorts, and we all work in the business. That includes aunts, uncles, cousins…all of us. Anyone could have stepped in…probably. Well, not my brother Theo, who makes Gordon Ramsey look like a preschool teacher. But all of us had worked at various levels of the business. Dad wanted me to take over and I couldn't let him down.

There was one thing that kept me from stepping down and letting my cousin Michael take over. Well two things. The first had been my father, who said he wanted me to take over. I never liked letting my father down, and I had a lot during those few years in my twenties after I graduated.

The second factor? Hazel Prescott.

Sure, Silas had been there, helping me along the way. I have an MBA, but I was a mess trying to deal with my mother, who had almost lost her soulmate, and several family members who had thought I wasn't smart enough to run the company. And when Silas started helping me, so did Hazel.

I knew being Silas' sister, she was smart, but I had not understood how crazy brilliant she is. All those late nights chatting about marketing, her telling me what to do to help our social media, all the brunches at Gertrude's…I just fell for her.

She's beautiful but she is also smart and one of the kindest people I know. And tonight, I will take my chance.

I step out of my bathroom and come to a stop. There standing in the family suite looking out over the city is my brother Theo. He's dressed to go out, in dark dress slacks and a red button-down shirt.

"What the hell are you doing here?"

"Hello to you too, brother," he says turning around. I see that he has a drink in his hand. He takes in my tux. "Well, don't you look spiffy."

I roll my eyes. I'm not in the mood for him, but it's not like I can avoid him. We don't hate each other, it's just that we're so different. People have always said there is a little darkness to Theo, which I don't understand. We were raised by the same parents, but he does seem to have an edge to him.

"Thanks. Are you going to the event?"

"To the fundraiser thing? Nope. I'm just irritated I got into the city and couldn't have the family apartment."

Our family has a suite at each one of our resorts just for family. I made sure to get this one set up as soon as I knew I would be here for the fundraiser. Since most of the family lives in the area, it rarely gets booked, but I wanted to be sure. Seems like I made the right choice. "Plus, I do not have a lady love who is running the whole thing."

"What?"

"Come on, Milo. Everyone knows you're in love with Hazel."

That makes me come to a stop. "Who is everyone?"

"Everyone. Mom has been dreaming of what your babies would look like. She even got Cousin Oliver to do one of those baby things where you load two pics into some software to see what a combo of you would look like. Beautiful, according to Mom, in case you were wondering."

Fuck. "Mom?"

"I'm sure Dad too. Everyone in the family, I think. I'm sure Silas knows you want to bang his sister."

My eyes narrow. "Watch it."

He gives me a smirk. "Sorry. Apparently, everyone but Hazel knows. Or I'm assuming."

I sigh. "That's embarrassing."

He shakes his head. "Don't be embarrassed. Just do something about it so Mom will be happy."

Then I realize it's a Saturday night and Milo is usually in the kitchen of our Shenandoah resort. As head chef, he rarely misses a Saturday night during the summer. It's really our busy time of year.

"What are you doing here anyway? You usually don't miss a Saturday night of work."

He's the typical chef who micromanages the entire kitchen and thrives on the challenge of running a Michelin star restaurant.

"I needed a break."

There's something in his voice that has me studying him. "What happened?"

"Nothing."

"Theodore."

"Ugh, don't use that name."

I chuckle knowing what probably happened. "What did you and Allegra fight about this time?"

Allegra Sullivan is the new food and beverage

manager for our resort. From the moment she started working there, Theo and she have been fighting. Strike that. They don't fight. She does what she thinks is best for the resort, then Theo complains to her about it. For only being twenty-five years old, she doesn't seem to have a problem dealing with his mood swings. She listens politely and then tells him to deal with it. It might have something to do with being the only girl with four brothers or having a Marine Corps officer for a father.

"She wants me to do some stupid social media thing where I prepare a meal on video."

"That's a good idea."

"And she thinks we should have cooking weekends to draw people in."

"Uh, Theo, you usually like being the center of attention."

He growls, setting the glass down on the dresser, and crosses his arms over his chest. Yes, he's temperamental, but he isn't childish, which this is. And I wasn't lying about him. He does like being the center of attention.

"True," he says. "But she said things that I didn't like about it."

He starts heading to the elevator that opens into the suite. I grab my phone and follow him because I need to know what's going on with him and Allegra.

"What kind of things?" I ask.

He doesn't say anything for a long moment. The door dings open, and we both get on the car.

"Theo."

He sighs. "She wants to do a lot of pictures because she said that women like a pretty piece of man meat."

I fight the bubble of laughter that tickles the back of my throat. "Did she say those exact words?"

He slants me a look. "Yeah. Well, that and something about sausages. I mean, what kind of woman talks like that?"

"Uh, some of the women you hook up with."

"No. This was…well, it made me feel dirty. I just never know what the hell she's going to do from one day to the next."

Before I can ask him more, the elevator doors open, and a rush of people come onto the car. We move to the back, and he gives me a look that tells me to drop the subject. We reach the ground floor, and I stop him before he can run away.

"Hey, if there's a problem between you and Allegra, we need to work it out."

"Or?"

"I'd hate to fire my brother."

He snorts. "Get bent, bro. Also, go get your woman. She'll be good for you."

He heads off down the hallway, something weighing on him as he walks. It isn't the usual dark cloud that seems to hang around him. It's something else and I do need to figure it out. But right now, I have more important things to worry about. Namely, Hazel.

I get to the ballroom where the event is being held and I step inside. It's already busy, less than an hour into the event and I know that has to be because of Hazel. She is a powerhouse at things like this.

It's then that I see her, talking to a gaggle of women. Hazel is easy to find. She's a head taller than most women and she's probably wearing some of her impossibly high stilettos. I love when she does because that puts our eyes level and I can just imagine bracing her against the wall as I drive into her again and again, all the while watching pleasure dance over her beautiful face.

It's then that I realize I'm getting an erection while standing in a room full of people. It's like I can't control myself, but maybe after tonight, I will at least gain some relief. Hopefully.

Watching her interaction makes me smile. She might think she doesn't fit in, but she does. They all seem to be in awe of her. She works hard at her job when she doesn't really need to, and she believes in her causes. This one for instance. The shelters it supports is massive and needs to have several fundraisers a year to keep afloat. I know that without a doubt, Hazel is instrumental in their ability to help so many people.

She's talking to Tracy Livingston, the sister of one of my older friends. Tracy says something to her, and she looks my way. The moment our gazes connect, it's like a fuse to my soul. The heat that was simmering explodes and rushes over every nerve ending in my body. It's like an itch that I can't reach. I can't seem to look away, and I don't want to. She's the most beautiful woman in the room.

Like Theo said, it's time to get my woman.

Chapter Seven

Hazel

My feet are killing me.

It's the only thing I can think about right now. There are fifty million things I need to be worried about: the silent auction, whether we are doing okay with open bars and food, and, of course, avoiding my ex. And Rachel. That woman has been by more than once to bug me. My phone buzzes in my hand and I look down.

Georgie: *Almost there.*

And Georgie! I almost forgot she was coming here. All I can think of are my poor feet.

I know, it's my fault because I insist on wearing heels. I'm five ten so I don't really need to wear them. Also, if I whine about my feet, then I can forget that Milo is coming here to pretend to be my boyfriend.

"Oh, wow, I had no idea that Milo Darling was going to be here."

My heart jumps as my entire body heats with need. I blink and look at Tracy Livingston.

"I had such a crush on him when we were in high school. He was friends with my brother," Tracy says.

I study her. She has always been beautiful in that girl next door kind of way. Blond curls are always perfectly styled, big brown eyes, and her make up never melts off her face. Plus, she's like a size 2. Don't get me wrong, I really like her and even though she was considered one of the most popular girls in our high school, she was also the sweetest. It's just that I always feel like a giant oaf next to her.

I look to where her attention is directed, and Milo is standing there looking over the crowd of people. The moment his gaze connects with mine, heat sparks low in my belly and I want to moan. This man, those amazing green eyes…they get to me every time. I squeeze my thighs together.

He makes his way over to where I'm standing, his gaze never leaving mine. There's a tickle in the back of my throat as I try to play it cool. I have never been that good at that, truth be told, but I promise myself I will do it tonight. I will be the cool girl.

Also, he should stop staring at me because now my nipples are hard, and I know they can be seen in this dress.

"He's coming this way," someone beside me says. I know it's not Tracy, but I know it's someone else who probably weighs ninety-five pounds.

I can practically hear all of them primping as he makes his way over to us. I know that I should probably do that, but I can't look away from him. People try to stop him, but he ignores them as he makes his way over to my group. Then he stops within inches of me.

"Hey, Hazel."

My mouth twitches, knowing that he's playing the role I designed for him. He could probably act on stage if his family's resorts go bankrupt.

"Milo."

"Hey, Milo," Tracy says.

He blinks and looks around like he hadn't noticed there were people standing nearby.

"Oh, Trace, how's your brother doing?" The heat that had been in his voice when he said my name is now gone.

"Fine. They just had another baby."

He nods and gives her a smile just as my favorite Dominion song starts playing. It's the ballad one of the band members wrote for his now wife. Milo's gaze comes back to me, and I might be imagining it, but they seem to soften. He knows this is my favorite song.

"I think this dance is mine," he says, letting one eyebrow rise.

I smile and take his offered hand and let him lead me out to the dance floor. He pulls me into his warmth, his natural scent surrounding me. God, he smells like sin and happiness all rolled up into one thing.

"You look amazing," he says. He's holding me so close; his lips graze my temple.

"Thank you," I say, amazed I found my voice. "You don't look so bad yourself."

He chuckles and the vibrations of it filter over my entire body. Oh, no. My nipples are so hard. I hope he can't feel them because I would be so embarrassed.

"Thank you," he murmurs, again his lips moving against my temple.

"Tracy has a crush on you."

"Who?"

"Tracy Livingston. She has a crush on you."

"Oh, Derrick's sister? Too young for me."

I lean back and look up at him. This close I can see the gold flecks in his eyes. His eyes are so light that they should look odd with his coloring, but they make him more mesmerizing.

"I'm the same age."

"Maybe I should say not mature enough. Girl still lives off her father."

"I work for my family's company."

"That's just it, you work. She doesn't. You're amazing and you run your own department. And you are as brilliant as you are beautiful. "

My mouth opens, then I snap it shut. What do I say to that? I didn't think he ever noticed me. I mean, other than being Silas' sister.

"Nothing to say?"

"I don't know what to say. You mean that?"

He blinks. "What's wrong with the men in this city? You should be told every day that you are a goddess."

"I'm not every man's cup of tea."

"That's a lie."

He is so vehement in his statement that I chuckle. "Not every man wants extra. And that's what I am." He opens his mouth to argue with me, but I stop him. "No. It's okay. I like myself, it's just that I understand I'm not what most men like."

"Well, they're idiots. Why would any man not want all the extra that you have?"

"I'm pushy."

"You're not."

"I'm tall and insist on wearing heels."

He leans forward and somehow; I feel as if he pulls me closer. I didn't think that was possible.

"When you wear those heels, they drive me crazy."

The words seem to rumble out of his chest. I draw back and look at him, shaking my head.

He nods.

I can't take him messing with me. I'm a grown woman who can usually navigate the insane attraction I have for him. I can pretend to be friends, and I can handle being the cute sister who is around for laughs. But tonight, I can't deal with it. Not when right now he looks so sincere.

I lean closer, and thanks to the heels I'm wearing, I can easily whisper in his ear. "Don't play with me, Milo. I know you're putting on a show for my friends, but I need you to be honest with me when we are alone."

I pull back and he's frowning at me. His hand at my waist slips a little close to my butt as he eases me even closer. It's then I feel him. Long, thick, and definitely hard, his erection is pressed against me. My eyes widen and he nods once, before leaning down to whisper in my ear, much like I just did to him.

"There is no pretending here, Hazel. If I didn't think you would go running from the room, I would tell you every fantasy I've had and all the ways I would love to use your body."

I shiver as my brain goes blank. Milo has thought of me that way? How? Why?

The song ends and he doesn't let go of me. He slips his finger beneath my chin, forcing me to look up at him. "Don't you have anything to say?"

For once, I ignore everyone and their whispers. Lord knows there are enough of them already, but us standing on the ballroom floor while another song starts up. I shake my head.

"Then I guess I'll take advantage of the situation."

Before I understand what that means, he dips his head and kisses me.

Chapter Eight

Milo

I slip my fingers up Hazel's jaw cupping it as I deepen the kiss. I've waited so long to have a taste of her, I don't ever want to stop kissing her. I trace the seam of her lips and she opens them, giving me a little moan that zeroes all the way to my balls as I dive inside of her mouth.

She tastes of wine and temptation. My entire body is vibrating with need for her, my dick is so hard I'm amazed I haven't passed out, and I want her now. I want to take her anywhere: upstairs, to the bathroom, to a dark corner. I want to plunge inside of her and feel all those little muscles cling to my cock as I ride her.

"Excuse me," someone says but I ignore him. Instead, I slip my hand down to Hazel's waist.

"Hey!"

I tear my mouth away from hers and growl at the person behind me. Fuck, it's that asshole Jason. He's a good two inches shorter than me, so with Hazel in heels, he's shorter than her at the moment as well. The sallow skin and bloodshot eyes tell me that he's still a drunk. He's the same age as Hazel, but he looks ten years older.

"I thought that was you, Hazel."

His eyes soften as he looks at her. I look at her. With swollen lips and flushed skin, she looks like she was thoroughly kissed, which she was. I look back at the asshole who interrupted us and have to fight the urge to step in front of her to block his view.

"Jason?"

"Yeah, Jason."

He steps closer to give her a kiss on the cheek but stops in his tracks when I growl.

"I-I wanted to have a chance to chat with you," he says.

"I'm a little busy right now, Jason."

Before he can open his mouth to insist, and before I can punch him, someone calls to Hazel.

"Sorry. I have to go take care of this before the silent auction happens." She ignores Jason and looks at me. "I'll be back in a bit."

"Hurry."

Her face flushes and she nods, then she hurries off. God, she's sexy. How she runs around in those heels of hers defies any explanation, but I find it so fucking sexy.

"I had no idea you and Hazel had a thing."

I turn to say something to him, but Silas steps up. "Well, why would you, bud? It's not like Hazel talks to you anymore." He turns to me and cuts off Jason. "Let's go get a beer," he says.

I nod and follow him, and even though I don't look back, I can feel Jason's gaze burning into my back. Silas says nothing as we make our way over to the bar. People don't try to stop us, because, you know, Silas. He doesn't like most people. Strike that. He doesn't like anyone but Georgie. He tolerates the rest of us. Once we have our beers, we step off to our own little corner.

"So," he says. I'm not fooled by his casual tone. I know that something else is coming.

"So."

He cuts a look my way and I wait for him to raise his objections to me dating his sister. No. Not dating. Marrying. Granted, I'm pretty sure that I can't say that to her right now. Hazel barely believes that I'm attracted to her. The fact that she didn't think I was attracted to her in truth when I was sporting a hard-on to end all hard-ons.

God, I can't wait to get her alone. I want to lick every bit of her body, taste her, watch her eyes go blurry when she comes.

Snapping fingers bring me out of my thoughts. I glance over at Silas, who is giving me a look of disgust. "Really?"

"Sorry. Your sister…" I shove a hand through my hair.

"What about my sister?"

"I don't care what you say, but I'm going to make this work."

"What I say? What do you mean?"

"I know I'm not good enough for her."

"Well, no, but then I'm not good enough for my Georgie."

I blink.

"I just want to say that it's about damned time. You've

been mooning over her forever. I told you the other day that I had no problems with this."

"I mean to marry her."

"Okay. I'm not the one you have to worry about."

"What do you mean?"

There is a little finger poke in my back. I turn around, then must look down at Georgie. She's dressed in a pink dress with a little sparkle to it. She's frowning at me, so she looks like a grumpy fairy.

"Yeah, you have to worry about me. I will ruin you if you hurt her heart."

I smile at her, which has her eyes narrowing as she crooks her finger at me. I lean down and she smacks me up against the head.

"Ow, dammit, Georgie."

"Don't cuss at my fiancé."

She rises up on her tiptoes. "I. Will. End. You."

Then she turns away and starts off in the direction of the silent auction. There's a bounce to her step as she flits about the room on her way to Hazel.

I turn to look at Silas, who is smiling after his fiancé. "She just threatened me."

"I know. It was fucking sexy."

I sigh and roll my shoulders before sipping at my beer.

"As I was saying, I'm for it. I know you've been in love with her for years."

"And?"

"I wouldn't mind having you for a brother."

I let loose a breath I hadn't known I had been holding onto. "Thanks, man."

"Now, I'm going to go after Georgie," he says,

wiggling his eyebrows at me. It is so out of character it makes me laugh. Well, it was before he met Georgie. He's still stuffy and doesn't always get jokes, but he has a different outlook on life these days.

I'm watching the back of the room where they are looking over the auction items. It's fascinating watching Hazel work. She's a bright light, happy and glowing, but I know better than to believe the surface. There are those who probably look at her and think she's a party girl like a lot of these women here. I have nothing against that, but for the woman I want by my side and in my bed.

Just then, I watch Jason approach her. Another growl rumbles in my chest as I watch him try to gain her attention by touching her. There is no fucking way I am going to let that happen.

Hazel

I t takes me about five minutes to be able to complete my job for the silent auction. Milo has no idea just how powerful his kisses are. I've been kissed before, but nothing like the one he laid on me a short while ago. I felt it all the way to my soul.

Once I get my brain in working order, I go through and double check all the descriptions for the articles that are about to be auctioned. I get in a groove and run through them pretty quickly. When I reach the last item, a weekend at a Darling Resort in the United States, I sense someone behind me. I turn with a smile on my face, which dissolves the moment I see Jason standing there.

"Hey, Haze. I thought we could catch up."

Jeez, the guy is a piece of work. He is so not under-standing that I want nothing to do with him. He's put on weight, and he's bloated. I heard he drinks a lot now. His weekend habit of getting blitzed has apparently spilled over into the week. And who the hell dresses him? I'm usually stuck up about clothes, but seriously, his tux looks like he slept in it.

What did I ever see in him?

"Why would we do that?"

He blinks. "What?"

"I'm asking why I would do that? I think we said everything we needed to say five years ago."

He broke up with me on my graduation day. We had been talking about moving in together, marriage, kids. Then we weren't.

"We didn't really talk it over."

I shake my head. "You were the one who broke up with me by text."

He didn't show up to my graduation and just sent me a message that said I was suffocating him. One of the happiest days of my life became a memory I would like to forget.

"That was stupid. I was stupid."

"You *were*?"

"Yeah."

"Oh, I was implying that you hadn't gotten any smarter over the years."

"I've been trying to come up with a way to approach you."

"Is this part of your twelve-step process? Apologizing?"

"What would I be apologizing for? We were growing apart for months."

That was news to me. "We'd been to look at apartments three days before you broke up with me. Then there was the fact that you were fooling around with Rachel."

"I was confused."

"Sounds like you really were," Milo says. The moment I hear his voice, my entire body shivers in anticipation. I glance over at him and notice he's watching me, his gaze on my mouth. I lick my lips in reaction, and he rolls his eyes and mutters something under his breath.

"Darling? What are you doing here?"

"I was just here to make sure that you weren't trying to make time with my girl."

"Your girl?" The way he says it makes me believe he doesn't really think we're together. I mean, we aren't, but that pisses me off.

"Yes, his girl," I say, my voice dripping with irritation. "I think we're done."

"I don't think we are," he says as he takes me by the elbow. I don't feel threatened, but I'm mad.

"We were done five years ago."

"But—"

"No buts. I'm done with you. I have been for years and why you're here makes no sense whatsoever."

"I…" he glances at Milo and for some reason, he pales. When I look over at my friend, I see the anger and have to fight to step back. I have never seen Milo angry before, and I know he would never hurt me. But he is definitely not a man anyone would want to anger.

"I thought we could catch up."

I frown. "What aren't you getting?"

Milo opens his mouth, but I hold up my hand to let him know that I have this. His mouth quirks, and he nods his head once to let me know that he will let me handle it.

"I don't want to be a with a man who was such a loser that the only way to break up with me was on text."

"It was too painful."

I roll my eyes. At him and at myself. There's a good chance five years ago, I would have fallen for that. I would have tried my best to smooth things over. But one thing I have learned over the last few years is that smoothing the situation over doesn't mean that things are okay.

"If it was too painful, then you should have stayed around."

"He was too busy," Rachel Burton says as she steps up next to him. She slips her arm through his.

She's dressed just this side of trashy. The dress she's wearing probably cost her more than five thousand dollars, but it's too gaudy, and a little too tight. Rachel is a pretty woman, with blond hair and a stick thin body, but she wears way too much makeup. She didn't used to look like this, but I sense she's panicking about getting married. There is also a venom about her I just don't get, but I don't like her mother much either, so the apple probably didn't fall that far from the bitchy tree.

I look at her, then at Jason as he tries to untangle himself from Rachel, but she seems to hold on tighter.

"Listen, this is all great, but I have things to do. The auction is about to start, and I haven't even had anything to nibble on. So, I am going to leave you two to figure out what the hell you are both talking about."

"Sounds good," Milo says, offering me his arm.

I take it and we go to the buffet tables. It isn't anything heavy, but there's a lot. And I realize then that I forgot to eat lunch. My stomach grumbles at the spread that's before us. I'm thankful for the music playing at that moment because I can't even think about how how embarrassed I would be if Milo heard my stomach rumbling.

We get a couple of plates and I think that he's going to find Silas and Georgie. Instead, he steers us toward a small table in a secluded corner. He waits for me to sit down before he does, after moving the chair closer to mine. In fact, I'm practically sitting in his lap.

"You know you don't have to do this."

He says nothing as he watches me pick up a shrimp and pop it into my mouth.

"I thought this is what we were doing?"

"Yes, but right now, who is paying attention?

He chuckles. I love his chuckle. It always makes me happy and warm inside.

"I think you forget who you are, sometimes." He leans closer so he can whisper in my ear. His breath feathers over my skin and I shiver. "Everyone is watching us right now."

I whip around and find out that he's right. I mean, they aren't openly staring, but they are throwing glances our way.

"You grab attention everywhere you go."

I look at him. "I think it has to do with you."

He shakes his head. "You don't see it, but people watch everything you do. You draw attention just by being yourself."

The way he says it makes the air back up in my lungs. It's like he admires me. I can feel myself falling into the trap. I have to keep reminding myself that this man is just doing a favor. He's playing a role.

"All the women were tittering about you."

"Doesn't matter."

"What do you mean?"

"The only woman I care about tonight is you."

I say nothing because I can't. He's staring into my eyes, holding my gaze hostage. The sincerity in his words pierce through all my barriers. I open my mouth to say something…anything, but my name is called up to the stage.

I blink, pulling myself out of the spell he cast on me.

"I gotta go."

He nods. "We'll finish this discussion later, Hazel."

It sounds like half promise, half warning. Just the thought leaves me a little freaked out. And a little horny.

"Okay."

It's all I can say before I rise and hurry off to do my job for the charity.

Chapter Ten

Milo

As the fundraiser winds down, I stand back and let Hazel finish up what she needs to do. I like doing this. It's something I discovered about myself tonight. I like being the one waiting on her. It makes sense since I feel like I've been waiting to make my move for years.

"Hey, Milo," a sultry voice says beside me. I glance over and see Belinda Michaels, a woman I hung around with in my early twenties. Truth of the matter was, I hung around a lot of women in my early twenties. I had a lot of fuck buddies, and a lot of it's hazy, thanks to my drinking. That's why I don't have more than one or two drinks. I wasn't an alcoholic, but I was on my way to being that way.

"Belinda," I say giving her a hug and a kiss on the cheek. "How have you been?"

"Okay, if you count my divorce as being okay."

I shake my head. "Sorry to hear about that."

"Yeah, well, he just didn't like to party that much and was talking about kids."

"Imagine that," I say, trying to keep sarcasm out of my voice, but knowing that I failed from the expression on her voice.

"Don't tell me you're thinking of getting serious with Hazel Prescott."

I do not like the way she says Hazel's name.

"I don't think you want to go there, Belinda."

"She's not your type at all, Milo. You like a party as much as I do."

It's been almost three years since I did any partying. "I do not like partying as much as I did back in the day. I have responsibilities."

"Is that why you're settling?"

Before I can answer, I feel a presence beside me, and I know that it's Hazel.

I can tell from her blank expression and pale skin that she heard Belinda.

"Belinda, nice to see you again."

"Of course," Belinda says. I notice that she doesn't reciprocate the greeting. I forgot how much of a cat she was.

"How's…what was his name? Oh, Dan. That's right. How is he doing?"

Belinda scowls. "We're getting a divorce."

"Oh…that's right," Hazel says in a tone that tells me she already knew about the divorce. "Dan told me when I talked to him on the phone a few days ago. He was very generous to give to the charity."

Belinda blinks and opens her mouth, but I put an end

to any sparring that might happen here. I'm not worried about Hazel. I'm more worried about what she would do to Belinda. Hazel is the sweetest woman in the world but come at her in a setting like this and she will destroy you. Then, she would feel bad about it later on.

"Are you ready to go, babe?"

She blinks and looks at me. "Uh, okay. Yes. I'm ready."

"See ya around, Belinda," I say, not meaning it at all. From the expression on her face, I can tell she knows it.

I hurry us away and toward the bank of elevators, and before Hazel can figure out what is going on, I get us on the lift, using my card to get to the apartment. She blinks as the elevator starts to rise.

"What are we doing here, Milo?"

"You left your stuff in the apartment, right? There was a bag there."

"Oh, yeah, I completely forgot about that. I can get it myself. The night is over. You don't have to do this."

I'm nervous and, well, so fucking hard at the moment, I don't know how my legs are functioning with no blood in my brain. So, I can't control my irritation. "Just shut up."

She blinks. "Excuse me?"

I can understand her reaction. She wasn't around in my drinking days. I was a real ass then, kind of preten-tious and I always acted like I owned the world.

"I am not doing this for you. I'm doing this for me."

"Milo, did you have too much to drink?"

I ignore that stupid question. Instead, aggravation and waiting for so long has me blurting out, "I did this for me because I want you more than I want my next breath."

She blinks up at me and before she can answer, the door opens to the apartment. I grab her hand and tug her off the elevator. She stumbles, and I catch her.

"I should take these things off," she says, looking down at her shoes. She twists her hand trying to get me to loosen my hold, but I tighten my hand.

She looks up at me, her eyebrows furrowed.

"Leave them on."

My voice has deepened, causing her gaze to shoot up to mine. I should try and be gentle, but I don't know if I can be delicate in explaining just how much I want to fuck her. I need to be inside of her."

"Milo? What is going on with you?"

I back her up against the wall. I press the lock on the elevator - my family is rude and wouldn't hesitate to interrupt us—and then crowd in closer. I release her hand, then place a hand on either side of her head.

I take a deep breath, and with the air comes the scent of her. She always smells like a field of roses, which I never thought I liked. That's until the first time I realized how much I loved Hazel.

"Wanna talk about what I just said?"

She blinks up at me and I want to fall into her eyes. She's a natural beauty and even on a night like tonight, she wore very little makeup. I love that she doesn't cover up her freckles.

"What part?"

"That I want you more than my next breath."

She closes her eyes and takes a long, deep breath. Her chest expands so that her nipples press lightly against my chest.

Fuck.

"Please don't play games with me, Milo. I can't take it." Her voice is small and she looks as if I manhandled her, she would break into a thousand pieces.

"Hazel," I say, my tone allowing for no argument. I can't help it. My dick is so hard, I'm ready to explode. There is no doubt in my mind that she can feel me. "Look at me."

When she raises her gaze, her eyes are filled with unshed tears. Seeing them is like a dagger to my heart. I cup her face with both of my hands.

"Why are you crying?"

She closes her eyes causing tears to stream down her face. Did I read her wrong? Did everyone? Georgie was convinced she felt the same way.

"Hazel, baby, please don't cry."

"I just…I know it was pretend tonight. You don't have to keep pretending."

I dip down and kiss her. "No pretending here, baby."

To prove my point, I press closer, enjoying the way her eyes snap open.

"Yeah, I've been hard since we danced tonight. Actually, since I saw you in that dress."

She shakes her head. "I get it. And I'm okay with one night. Just don't lie to me. I can't take it."

I frown. "This isn't about one night."

"Milo, I'm not the kind of woman a guy like you goes for."

"What the actual fuck are you talking about? A woman like you? You are *exactly* the kind of woman I would go for."

She rolls her eyes. "I've seen the pictures from when you used to party. I know the kind of women you were seen with then. Women like Belinda."

I hate that she seems to be shrinking in stature as she keeps speaking.

"Sure, I dated on the party scene, of course, I was drunk most of the time, so my tastes were not as discerning as right now."

She rolls her eyes. "Please don't use that kind of line on me. It doesn't work on me anymore."

I hear the pain in her voice and once again I feel it cut through me. "Who said that to you?"

I know even before she says his name, but I need to hear it from her.

"It doesn't matter." She isn't even looking at me and it pisses me off. My heart might be bleeding for her, but the fact that she's allowing that asshole to ruin what we could have irritates me.

"Look at me."

She hesitates, that lower lip coming out and I want to laugh—but it would hurt too much.

She finally raises her eyes.

"Tell me."

"Jason. He used it when we were in college. Said I wasn't like the other girls."

It's true. She isn't like them but from her tone, she thinks that's a bad thing. It isn't.

"He's an asshole."

She nods. "I know that now, but the fact that I was that stupid all those years ago, it just…"

"You were in your early twenties. Ask me what I was doing at that point in my life."

She rolls her eyes once again.

"I can't tell you. I can't remember a lot of it because I was partying all that time. Until my dad had the heart attack. Then, everything went to shit."

I hadn't spent enough time learning the business when I had to take it over. Hazel knows this because without Silas and her by my side helping, I would have floundered and lost our entire business.

"No one else stood by me. All those party people disappeared, and you were there."

"Silas too."

"Silas isn't as good at marketing as you. You're the one who helped me. And you want to know what I discovered?"

She nods.

"I found a best friend, and also the love of my life."

Her eyes widen. "What?"

"I've been in love with you forever, Hazel Prescott. I might just die if you don't love me back."

Chapter Eleven

Hazel

For a long moment, my brain stops functioning. Milo loves me? How is that even possible?

"I'll tell you how that's possible," he growls out. My eyes focus and find him staring down at me. Damn, I can't believe I said that out loud.

Also, that growly voice? It turns me on. My panties are already wet, and my nipples, well, they are so hard I know he can see them through the soft fabric of my dress. I cross my arms over my breasts to hide them, but the friction makes it worse.

"I'm waiting." I try for haughty, but I come off sounding like some kind of sex crazed chick. Even I can hear the heat in my voice.

"You are the most amazing woman, Hazel. If I had known you didn't know, I would have told you every damned day. You have a stunning mind."

"Oh, yeah, men love that. That's why *Sports Illustrated* has a bunch of female physicists on their cover." I don't hide the sarcasm. I've been told more than once that I'm too smart for my own good and usually from men.

"This man does and I'm the only one that matters." Oh, God, he's going all growly again. This is not good for my panties. They're drenched and getting worse every time he gets like that.

"I'm waiting for more."

"Your kind heart, the way you love your family, and Christ, woman, you make my dick hard just standing there frowning at me."

I blink.

"Yeah. I've spent every moment with you trying to fight my attraction to you."

"Why on earth would you do that?"

He sighs and for the first time, he looks vulnerable. "I didn't think I was good enough for you."

It takes my brain a moment to catch up with the words that just came out of his mouth. "What on earth are you talking about?"

"I wasn't a good man in my early twenties. I slept around a lot, and I was lazy. I..." He looks away for a moment as if trying to gather the courage to tell me he has a secret family in South Dakota. When he turns back to look at me, all I can see is honest admiration. "You weren't like that."

He looks embarrassed by the admission. I never thought he had any feelings for me, especially not ones that made him feel badly about himself. For a second, I study this man, the one I have loved for so long, not only for his beauty but also for the way he acts towards others. He might have been lazy and not so good in his early twenties, but he's a good man now.

I cup his face with both of my hands and look into his eyes. I love this man more than life itself and I'm sick of hiding it.

I lean forward and brush my mouth over his before diving into his mouth. Our tongues tangle, his hands go to my hips, pulling me fully against him. Oh, God, he's so hard. His hands slip from my waist down to my rear end, lifting me off the ground. I wrap my legs around him, and he groans against my mouth.

Before I know what's happening, I find my back against the mattress. He covers me with is body. It feels so good to have his weight against me, to have his cock nestled between my thighs.

Milo settles his weight on his hands on either side of my head. "Tell me."

I know what he wants, what he needs. And I need to say it, to tell him just how I feel. I slip my hands from his shoulders to cup his face once again. "I love you, Milo Darling. I have for the longest time."

For a second, he says nothing, just stares down at me. Then, a smile curls his lips. It is the most beautiful smile I've ever seen in my life.

"Good, because I am never letting you go."

That comment has my brain intervening. I can't just give everything over to him, can I? If I start believing in forever again, and I don't get it, what happens then? When I was with Jason, I thought it was forever, but that was before I fell for Milo. The love I have for him is nothing compared to those feelings I had for my ex. They consume me and make me feel the most vulnerable I have ever felt.

I open my mouth, not sure what to say, but he takes care of that for me. He cups my face, slanting his mouth over mine and demolishes any of the objections I had. Before I can respond to that, he's kissing me again and I'm lost in the moment.

Milo tears his mouth away from mine and kisses down my neck, then pulls away. I frown at the loss of his body heat, but he doesn't give me time to argue. Instead, he slips off the bed, manhandles me until I'm on my stomach. Then he straddles me.

"This dress…it just about killed me; you know? I almost came in my pants when I saw you."

Oh, God, he's going to kill me. I figure the cheeky panties I'm wearing are probably ruined. He kisses my neck, then moves down, unzipping the back of my dress as he does.

"I was so angry too."

"Wait, what? You were mad that I almost made you come?"

He chuckles, a puff of his breath skating over my sensitive flesh. "No, goddess. It was that every man in there wanted you. I saw the looks you got."

"Have you been drinking?"

He stills, then pulls away from my back. The next thing I feel is his palm smacking my rear end. I yelp from the sharp sting, but in the next instant, I feel another gush of arousal. Oh, no. I like spanking. I squirm and realize the heat of the slap sent my arousal to another level.

Milo picks up on it right away. "Oh, so my goddess

likes spanking. Hmm. Never been one of my things, but now…well, let's just say I *will* be shopping for paddles."

His voice deepens over every word he speaks. I can hear the arousal in his voice, which of course sends another wave of need slapping through my entire body.

"Now, back to talking about this dress and getting you out of it."

His hand is on the zipper again. His mouth is on my back, kissing each inch of skin he reveals. He moves slowly, taking his time, driving me crazy. I want him now, like hard and fast, but he isn't going to give me that.

I squirm, and he chuckles. By the time he has it completely unzipped, every nerve ending in my body is sizzling.

"I need your arms out of the dress."

His voice is rougher, need skating along his vocal cords. I have the bodice down and he's tugging the dress off me.

After he gets it completely off, silence descends on the room. This can't be good. I could lay there and wonder if he is disgusted by what he sees, but I can't take it. I need to know. I pull myself up, resting my weight on my arms so I can turn around to look at him.

His gaze is practically devouring my body, taking in every inch,

"Fuck me," he says, his voice just barely above a whisper. "If I had known you looked like this, I wouldn't have lasted as long as I did."

I blush, seriously blush, as he looks up at me. "I called you a goddess, but I had no idea. I mean…damn."

Milo Darling, delectable bachelor is speechless looking

at me. Happiness moves through me, power rushing through my blood that makes me bold. I roll over onto my back. He groans.

"What's the matter, Milo?"

"I…" again he's at a loss for words.

"What?"

"Listen, I have spent so much time imagining this for the last few years, but my fantasies didn't even get close to the reality. You are a work of art."

Normally I would disagree, but his tone stops me. He truly believes I am a goddess."

"You had fantasies about me?"

He nods, his gaze connecting with mine. "So many times. I know this is crass, but I came so many times imagining this."

I'm sure there are other women who would be disgusted by that admission, but it just turns me on. I sit up and my hands go to my shoes.

"Nope, I want those on the first time I fuck you."

The command should make me upset, but instead, it shoots right to my pussy.

"Fine, but I would like to get a little view of you too."

His mouth kicks up on one side and I feel my heart turn over. This man is so pretty, so delectable, I don't know how this is even happening. But, right now, I don't care. I'm just going to live in the moment.

His hands go to the bowtie that he undoes easily. Before I know it, he's standing in front of me in nothing but a pair of knit boxer briefs. The outline of his hard cock easy to see. He's so fucking big; I can see the tip peeking out from the waistband. Next, his boxers go, and he wraps his hand around his thick cock. It's not only long, but it's thick.

Fuck me.

My gaze flies up to his.

"Don't worry, goddess, it will fit." He joins me back on the bed, easily undoes the front closure of my bra and slides my cheeky panties off.

"Please tell me this is what you wear all the time," he says, holding them up as he kneels on the mattress. "If not, I am going to start shopping for them."

Milo Darling wants to buy me panties. That is possibly the weirdest sentence I have ever thought.

He settles down between my legs, his mouth skimming the flesh just above the top of my stockings. "I love these," he says. "That and your shoes. I love the way you prance around in them as if you're walking on air. So many times, I imagined showing up at your office, bending you over your desk, and taking you from behind while you were wearing a pair of them."

I shiver as his breath dances over my pussy. He licks my slit, humming as he does it. "Tastiest pussy around."

That's the last thing he says for a while because in the next moment, his tongue slips inside of me, and I lose it. Milo is more than a little talented with his tongue, as he slips his hands under my ass to pull me up off the mattress. The way he's holding me, I have no control over anything. I am at his mercy and, truthfully, I don't care.

He fucks me with his mouth, pushing me closer and closer to the edge. But something is holding me back. I don't know what it is, but he lets out a frustrated growl. He pulls away and looks up my body at me, licking his lips.

Oh, God, he's gorgeous. Then, he does something I don't expect. He repositions himself, letting go with one of his hands, then smacks my pussy.

At first, I'm so stunned, I don't say anything. The next one he gives me sends heat searing through my blood and does something to loosen the tension I was holding onto.

With a satisfied look, he dips his head again, this time sucking on my clit while slipping two fingers into me. It has been a long time since I had sex, but I'm so wet it makes it easier for him.

And before I know it, I am flying over the edge as he continues to tease me through my orgasm. Then, he's pulling away and kissing his way up my body and devouring my mouth. I can taste myself there, and I love it.

He freezes. "Fuck."

"What's wrong?"

"I forgot condoms. It's been so long."

I cup his face. "I'm on the pill and I haven't been with anyone in years."

"I'm clean. It's been a long time for me."

I smile. "I want you inside me, Milo. Now."

He groans and kisses me again. Positioned at my entrance, he pushes inside of me. It has been a while, and he's huge, but I enjoy each inch he sinks into me. Once he's fully seated to the hilt, he draws himself up to his knees, dragging me with him. Then, he starts to move. Fast, hard, deep thrusts. I feel another orgasm building, my muscles tensing, anticipation rising each time he thrusts inside of me.

"Come on my dick, goddess. I want to feel all those muscles pulling on me."

As if my body can't do anything but follow his directions, I come again, closing my eyes and screaming his name. I see stars as pleasure courses over me. He thrusts two more times before groaning.

"Yeah, fuck, goddess, so good," he groans, as his fingers dig into my flesh, and he pours himself into me.

He collapses a few seconds later and apologizes.

"Don't," I say, wrapping my arms around him. Nothing could have been as perfect as this. He pulls up, kisses my nose, then pulls out of me. He helps me out of my shoes and stockings, then we toss the comforter and slip under the sheets. He pulls me against him, my back against his chest.

"Good night, goddess," he murmurs arounds my neck. His breathing evens out a few seconds later, but I don't fall asleep right away. I know he said that he might think he loves me, but tomorrow is a different day.

I will never regret what we did. Even if he wants to pretend it never happened, I will always cherish this night we had together.

Milo

The soft sunlight is peeking through the curtains. Usually, I hate mornings, but not this morning. That's because of the woman in my bed. I study her sleeping. She's always in motion, so watching her still and dreaming, it's something new for me. I want it every morning of the rest of my life. Her dark curls are spread out against the white sheet, and I cannot wait to see her in my bed in my house. I want her there, with me every morning. Just the thought of spending my life with this woman, building a family, has my dick twitching.

Inwardly, I sigh. This woman has no idea just how much she controls me. I took her twice more last night and early this morning. I'm like some damned rutting bull who can't go long without his dick surrounded by her warm heat.

"You know it's creepy that you're staring at me like that, right?"

Humor lights her voice, but there is a sleepy sexiness that permeates it. Fuck, this woman.

I brush some of her dark hair away from her face. Her eyes blink open, and I will remember this moment for the rest of my life. The first morning Hazel Prescott—soon to be Darling—woke up in my bed.

"What's that look for?"

"Thinking about things."

"Oh? What kind of things?"

"Things like if you are going to keep your name or take mine."

When she doesn't smile at me, I frown.

"What's that about?" I ask, trying to keep the worry out of my voice. I fail miserably.

"What?"

She's looking everywhere but at me.

"What? I just told you we're getting married."

"First of all, no man tells me what to do. Second of all, you did not. You mentioned last names."

"What the fuck do you think that means?"

"Listen, Milo, I understand—"

"If you think I made love to you last night and am going to let you walk away today, that's some bullshit. You told me you loved me."

"I do love you."

Truth rings out of her voice and shines in her eyes. That settles my nerves a little, but even so, I am not liking this situation. She is still avoiding eye contact, and I have a feeling what this is about. Hazel is a woman who needs concrete evidence of what I feel. I thought I gave her that last night, but that asshole did a number on her.

Without saying anything, I slip out of bed, then walk over to her side. Her eyebrows furrow as she looks up at me, but I remain mum. Instead, I lean forward and grab her, yanking her out of bed naked. I toss her over my shoulder in a fireman hold.

"Milo!"

I ignore her irritation and take her to the bathroom. I set her down on her feet and turn her to look at herself in the mirror. I can see love bites all over her body. I should be ashamed of doing that, but I like seeing my mark on her. I also see whisker burn. All of it shows ownership and I love that.

What I also see, and I need her to see, is how I think of her. She is the most beautiful woman on the planet.

"Milo, why are we here?"

"We're here because you need to understand just how I think of you, well beyond that beautiful brain and bright heart of yours."

Her gaze meets mine in the mirror. Her eyes go dreamy, telling me I must have said the right thing. I'm so fucking hard I want to plunge into her hot, wet cunt, but I know we need to get the air cleared.

"Now, look at yourself. Look."

She sighs and forces her gaze to the mirror. I move her hair back over her shoulders, so she can see her tits without obstruction. Okay, that was more about me seeing them.

"Do you see what I see? The love bites when I couldn't control myself, my whisker burn between your legs. You might not see that, but I know you feel it."

"Yeah, but—"

"Shut it."

Her eyes flare, irritation darkening them. Damn, this woman is sexy.

"I'm sorry, but I can't have you diminish how much I love you. How much I spend of my day thinking about you, about eating that sweet pussy of yours. Lord knows it's going to be worse now that I've actually had a taste of it. Now I'll fantasize about you most of the day and get nothing done, but that's okay. You're worth it."

"Indeed?"

I can't tell if she's pissed. Her voice is neutral.

I slip one hand around to her belly, then slide it down to her pussy. "Yeah. You have no idea what it felt like to get inside of you. All warm, and tight."

I skim my index finger over her slit while I grab her hair in my other hand, tugging on it so I can get access to her neck.

"You see how wet you are?" I slide one finger inside of her, then use my thumb to press against her clit. "Oh, yeah, my goddess loves that."

Her muscles ripple against my digit. It's too much for me. I pull away from her and spin her around, kneeling in front of her. I use no finesse, just put my mouth on her hot cunt. Fuck, she tastes just as delectable as the night before. Her tangy sweet flavor slips over my taste buds and I feel a little precum seep out of my dick. I slip my tongue in again, before adding two fingers, then run the tip of my tongue over her clit. She comes fast and hard, her fingers in my hair, as she screams my name.

I rise to my feet, turn her around, positioning her just how I want her, and thrust into her from behind. She has to lean forward, her breasts pressing against the cold counter. I'm ruthless, needing to get her off again, wanting to be right there with her when she comes.

I grab her hair and pull on it a little bit. She moans and I smile. My goddess likes it a little rough and I'm happy to give it to her.

I release her hair and spank her ass, her muscles contract around my dick. Fuck, she really does like a spanking.

My balls grow heavy as I feel my orgasm approaching, but I need to wait, to make sure she is with me.

"Hazel, goddess, look at yourself. Look how sexy you are."

She doesn't open her eyes, so I spank her once more, enjoying the way her skin turns pink.

"Open your eyes."

I watch her struggle, but she finally opens her eyes.

"Yeah, that's you. Fuck, you are the sexiest woman alive, and I don't think I ever want to stop fucking you. I want you beneath me, on top of me, anywhere. I want you always and you are just going to have to get used to it."

Hazel's gaze meets mine in the mirror, and I see it there. The realization of my feelings. That I am not lying.

I know my fingers are digging so deep that I will probably leave bruises, but I can't control myself. I am slamming into her hard, and I'm dancing on the edge of pure bliss.

"Come for me, goddess. Do. It. Now."

That is apparently enough. With her gaze on mine in the mirror, she comes, her body convulsing, as she bucks up against me. I slam into her one more time and I come, pleasure sparking through every bit of my body. My eyes roll back in my head as I pour myself into her. It's then I have a fleeting thought that I can't wait to do that without her on the pill. I want babies with this woman and the sooner the better.

I kiss her shoulder before pulling out of her to start the shower. I turn back to her find her watching me.

"What?"

"You are amazing Milo Darling."

"Only because I have you, goddess," I say stepping closer and picking her up into my arms. "And right now, I really want to try out this shower."

She gives me a blinding smile and it has my heart skipping a beat. "I agree."

After a shower where she lets me wash her hair, we make love again, this time with her back against the shower glass as I pound into her.

We stumble back to the bed, and I pull her into my arms.

"Do we have anywhere to be today?" Hazel asks, her sleepy voice making me smile.

"Right here, goddess. Just right here together."

Forever.

Epilogue

HAZEL

1 year later

I feel the soft, warm breeze dance over my flesh as I slowly wake up. The scent of plumeria is heavy in the air that's tinged with the scent of salt. It takes me a moment to completely wake up and remember where I am.

Hawaii.

We're on the island of Kauai, Princeville to be exact.

He proposed to me three months after he moved in with me. Granted, the move happened the week after our first night together. He just showed up one day with a bunch of clothes and that was that. Not that I'm complaining. From the moment we got together that night at the fundraiser, we just clicked. We've had our disagreements, don't get me wrong. But in the end, we want to be together, and that's what matters.

Our wedding had been held at their Shenandoah resort. We waited this long because I wanted to have enough time in between Silas and Georgie's wedding and ours.

It's been less than forty-eight hours since we were married. I snuggle deeper into Milo's embrace. It's not even dawn yet, but I have found that when I arrive here in Hawaii, I wake up before the sun does. It's annoying but being that I love the reason for our visit, I'm not complaining.

Milo moves his mouth over my neck, kissing his way up to my ear. His cock is hard against my ass.

"Good morning, Mrs. Prescott-Darling. How are you feeling this morning?"

"Fine and dandy."

He chuckles and the deep, happy sound dances through me.

"Is that a fact? How about if," he says, slipping his fingers inside of me, "we start out with something to make you even happier?"

I hum because his fingers are pumping in and out of me. A year later, it's still like this. All he has to do is touch me, and I want to jump him.

Before I can come, he pulls his fingers out, lifting my leg up and back over him, so that he can enter me from behind.

I moan because we have been doing little else other than making love since we got here. I'm tender, but I don't care. Having his dick deep inside me is the best feeling in the world. He goes easy on me, apparently understanding, but it doesn't take us long. He knows my body so well and can almost get me to come on command.

Waves of pleasure wash over me as my orgasm breaks free. Milo follows me a few seconds later.

Afterwards, we lay there, happy to just spend this time together. We have both been busy over the last year with work and with my charity. Darling Resorts is now a full partner in my Safe Haven Charity. It's something so fantastic to work with the man I love on something so important. He is great at coming up with different ways to raise money using their hotels.

He has his arms wrapped around me and I have never felt this safe in my life.

"It's hard to believe," he says, kissing the top of my head.

"What is?"

"That you married me. That you're mine forever and ever."

I lean back and look up at him. "It was meant to be, Milo."

His mouth quirks and it's then I have to tell him my secret. I've been keeping it from him for two weeks, but with the wedding and everything else, I didn't want to bring it up.

"You remember when we talked about kids?"

He nods kissing my forehead. "Of course."

"How would you feel about having one in about seven months from now?"

"That would be kind of hard to do because you would have to be…"

He voice trails off, as he looks down at me.

Tears fill my eyes. "Yeah. Seven months."

"How long have you known?"

"Just about ten days. I wanted to tell you, but I didn't want to tell anyone else first. I wanted it to be just us."

He says nothing. He just continues to stare at me.

"Milo, say something."

"Goddess…I…" he swallows, then his mouth curves into the biggest smile I've ever seen. "You're going to make me a dad."

He kisses me then, through the tears that are now running down my cheeks.

"Don't cry, goddess. I can't take that."

"They're happy tears."

"Still, I can't have my woman crying, not when she gives me the best news of my life."

He brushes the tears away before kissing me again, but he starts pressing kisses on my neck, urging me onto my back. He kisses, bites, and licks his way down my body. He settles his big body between my legs, pressing my thighs apart.

"Let me show you just how happy I am about it."

Milo

We spend most of our days on our honeymoon in bed or on the beach. I'm at the family's private residence on the island, and we opted not to have servants or cooks or anything. I gave them the week off with pay. Three days after she told me I am going to be a dad, we're sitting on the lanai sipping our coffee. Well, I am drinking coffee, she's having some decaffeinated tea. I'm just thankful she didn't turn into the exorcist that Georgie did during her pregnancy.

My phone buzzes and I ignore it until I see Theo's message.

Theo: *911*

Fear hits me first. Ever since my father's heart attack a few years ago, we promised to keep each other apprised of what is going on with our parents. Apparently, my father had had several "issues" before the heart attack that almost killed him.

I call him right away on video.

He answers immediately. His face is red, and murder darkens his eyes.

"You have to fire her."

"Hello to you too," I say sarcastically.

"Quit being a dick. You have to fire her."

I don't have to ask who he's talking about. He and my food and beverage manager still haven't learned to get along.

"No. Now, I'm going back to my honeymoon."

"Then I quit."

"Okay."

"Wait, what?"

"Listen, Theo, you are almost thirty. You need to learn to play nice with others."

"Why do you like her so much?'

"Because she has increased our profits by fifty percent. Just last month I caught the Brandon Resorts trying to poach her."

Irritation is replaced by rage. "What the fuck?'

"Yes, they know how good she is. She turned them down because she's loyal."

I don't miss the way he relaxes once he realizes she isn't leaving. "She's horrible."

I roll my eyes. "Did you really just call me on my honeymoon to complain about a woman?"

"She's not a woman."

"She's not?"

"You know what I mean. I don't see her that way."

I actually think he's lying. He sees her that way and it drives him crazy.

"And I did wait until the sun was up there."

Hazel gets up to get into the shot. "Hey, Theo."

His frown softens to a mini scowl. "Hey sis. How are you feeling?"

We told our families a couple of days ago about the baby. We thought about waiting until we got back to the mainland, but we just couldn't wait.

"I'm feeling fine, but apparently you are still having problems with Allegra."

"She…let's just say she has to go."

"What is this really about?" she asks as I urge her into my lap.

"I…well, she said horrible things about my cooking."

I almost laugh, but I don't. I know that Theo's whole identity is wrapped up in his ability to cook. He's been in the kitchen since he was five. It just came naturally to him. So, hitting him there is definitely picking at his ego.

"I bet you two were in a fight," I say, knowing that I am stating the obvious.

"That is the perpetual state of our working relationship."

"You need to learn to work with her."

"No."

Just that. No. And rudely said to my goddess.

"I think you need to dial back your attitude, Theodore."

He makes a sound of disgust and I know it's the name again.

"Theo, just get to know her. She's a little bossy," Hazel says gently. She is so much better at this than I am. I just want to tell him to fuck off and act like an adult.

"That's the understatement of the decade."

"But it comes from her upbringing. Did you know she is the youngest of five kids and all the others are boys?"

"Yeah."

"And her father was a bit of a terror, she said."

His eyes narrow. "In what way?"

"Just, rules. They had a very structured life as a Marine family. So, it's probably hard for her to deal with sharing responsibilities, especially with a man. Being the youngest and only girl, she has her issues with fitting in."

He grumbles but I can't make it out.

"What was that?"

"Fine. I won't quit."

"Good," I say. "You have any other problems; they can wait until we return next week."

I end the call without waiting for an answer.

"Milo," Hazel says with a giggle. "That was mean."

"So is calling up to bitch at me about a woman while

I'm on my honeymoon. I wish he would just give up the fight."

"Oh, so you see it too, right? I mean, those two definitely have the hots for each other."

He shrugs. "I don't care. All I care about is you, and that bed," I say, slipping my arm beneath her legs and rising from the chair. I step into the bedroom.

"Yeah? What about that bed?"

I nibble on her mouth as I make my way over to it.

"I want to test out those springs again."

She's laughing as we fall together on the bed and ignore the world outside of the room. Together forever and always.

Have you checked out the first book in the series???

1-Click Today —>Faking it with my Billionaire Boss

***Omg another hit!! Instalove and intsagreat!!*-**Rachel, Goodreads Review

***Their passion sizzled off the pages… -**Phuong, Goodreads

***…great characters, intense attraction and a storyline that pulls you in.*-**Kimberly, Goodreads

Download Today—>Faking it with my Billionaire Boss

Coming Next–>

Don't miss the exciting conclusion to the Faking it Series!

Preorder Today

Dealing with Theo Darling is possibly the worse job I've ever had in my life.

I get it. He's a genius in the kitchen--and out of it from

what I hear. The problem is, he knows it. He knows that he is an amazing chef. He knows that while I am the food and beverage manager, his family owns the resort. He has an ego bigger than any man I have ever met, and that includes my four older brothers. We're opposites in every way.

I need order and he lives in chaos. I like to adhere to a strict schedule. Theo...does not. In any way. It's amazing that we haven't killed each other yet.
Except when those annoying brothers I mentioned blow into town with a friend they want me to date and Theo rescues me. Sure, we can pretend to be attached for just a couple days. And sure, pretending to kiss him feels a whole lot like real kisses.

And when he whispers my name against my skin...let's just not go there.

Because, while my brothers will be out of my hair soon enough, I'm not sure I will never forget what it felt like pretending to be Theo's, even for just a few days.

Author Note: This tough as nails military brat heroine is about to have her world turned upside down. There's inappropriate behavior at work, a chef who knows how to use his hands, bickering, and four older brothers who will irritate our heroine to no end. As always, there is a happily ever after for our hero and heroine. I just make them suffer a little to get it ;)

SAME WORLD. ANY ORDER. INDIVIDUAL LOVE.

Introducing the Melissa Schroeder Instalove Collection. All books are in the same world but can be read in any order as they are stand alones. All books are low on drama, high on heat, and a have happily ever after. Look for the Instalove stamp whenever you want a short, fun, sexy story.

From an early age, USA Today Best-selling author Melissa loved to read. When she discovered the romance genre, she started to listen to the voices in her head. After years of following her AF Major husband around, she is happy to be settled in Northern Virginia surrounded by horses, wineries, and many, many Wegmans.

Keep up with Mel, her releases, and her appearances by subscribing to her NEWSLETTER or join in the fun with her Harmless Addicts!

Check out all her other books, family trees and other info at her website!

If you would want contact Mel, email her at:

melissa@melissaschroeder.net

instagram.com/melschro

amazon.com/author/melissa_schroeder

facebook.com/MelissaSchroederfanpage

twitter.com/melschroeder

bookbub.com/authors/melissa-schroeder

goodreads.com/Melissa_Schroeder

- Interest
- Series
- Entire Backlist